n be worked in cross stitch on
ida and using TWO strands of
e cross stitch and ONE strand for
s possible to work it on different
e number of strands used.

es first and then the backstitching,
s and colours shown.

DMC stockist for more
Woodland World. For your
ease phone:
on 01162 811040.

BACK STITCH

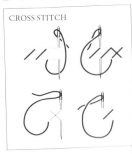

CROSS STITCH

GW00802305

Kingdom in 1995 by

Bridge Road, London SW1V 2SA
Reg. No. 954009

dom House UK Ltd 1995
995
orld, Leicestershire

WOODLA

BIRTHD

The design shown ca
Zweigart 14 count A
DMC stranded for th
the backstitching. It
fabrics by varying the

Work the cross stitch
following the symbol

Please see your local
needlework kits from
nearest UK stockist p
DMC Creative World

First published in the United
Ebury Press Stationery
Random House, 20 Vauxhall
Random House UK Limited

1 3 5 7 9 10 8 6 4 2

Set in Perpetua
Printed and bound in Singapore
Designed by Peter Butler

ISBN 0 09 180926 6

EBUR

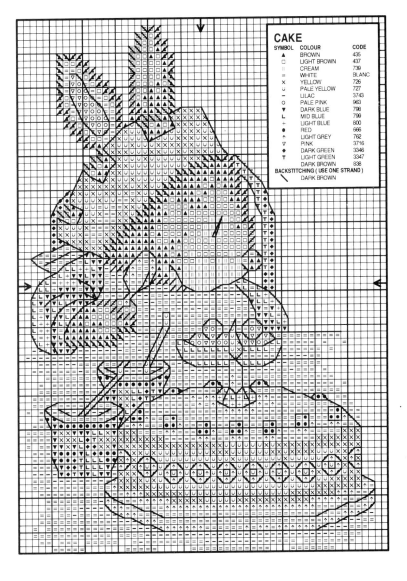

CAKE

SYMBOL	COLOUR	CODE
▲	BROWN	435
□	LIGHT BROWN	437
‖	CREAM	739
=	WHITE	BLANC
×	YELLOW	726
∪	PALE YELLOW	727
−	LILAC	3743
○	PALE PINK	963
▼	DARK BLUE	798
L	MID BLUE	799
+	LIGHT BLUE	800
●	RED	666
^	LIGHT GREY	762
▽	PINK	3716
◆	DARK GREEN	3346
T	LIGHT GREEN	3347
	DARK BROWN	838

BACKSTITCHING (USE ONE STRAND)

| \ | DARK BROWN |

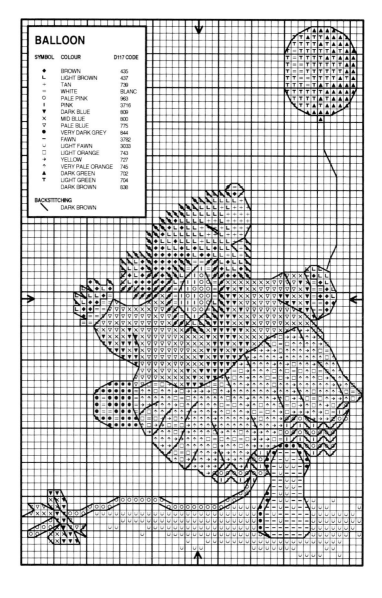

BALLOON

SYMBOL	COLOUR	D117 CODE
◆	BROWN	435
L	LIGHT BROWN	437
+	TAN	739
=	WHITE	BLANC
○	PALE PINK	963
I	PINK	3716
▼	DARK BLUE	809
×	MID BLUE	800
▽	PALE BLUE	775
●	VERY DARK GREY	844
—	FAWN	3782
∪	LIGHT FAWN	3033
□	LIGHT ORANGE	743
→	YELLOW	727
∧	VERY PALE ORANGE	745
▲	DARK GREEN	702
T	LIGHT GREEN	704
	DARK BROWN	838

BACKSTITCHING
    \   DARK BROWN

JANUARY

1

2

3

4

5

JANUARY

6

7

8

9

10

JANUARY

11

12

13

14

15

JANUARY

16

17

18

19

20

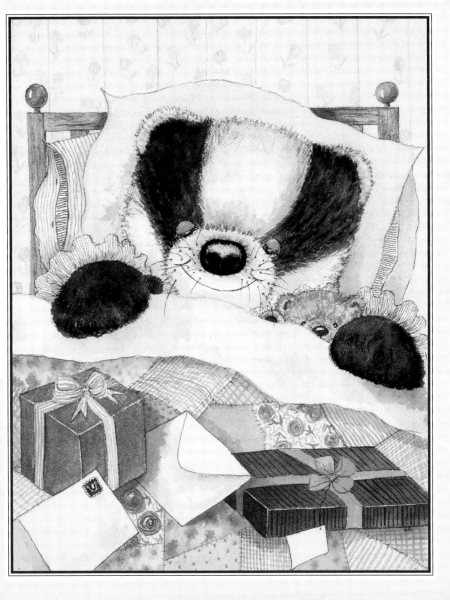

JANUARY

21

22

23

24

25

JANUARY

26

27

28

29

30

31

1

2

3

4

FEBRUARY

5

6

7

8

9

FEBRUARY

10

11

12

13

14

FEBRUARY

15

16

17

18

19

FEBRUARY

20

21

22

23

24

FEBRUARY

25

26

27

28

29

MARCH

1

2

3

4

5

MARCH

6

7

8

9

10

MARCH

11

12

13

14

15

MARCH

16

17

18

19

20

MARCH

21

22

23

24

25

MARCH

26

27

28

29

30

MARCH–APRIL

31

1

2

3

4

APRIL

5

6

7

8

9

APRIL

10

11

12

13

14

APRIL

15

16

17

18

19

APRIL

20

21

22

23

24

APRIL

25

26

27

28

29

30

1

2

3

4

MAY

5

6

7

8

9

MAY

10

11

12

13

14

MAY

15

16

17

18

19

MAY

20

21

22

23

24

MAY

25

26

27

28

29

MAY–JUNE

30

31

1

2

3

JUNE

4

5

6

7

8

JUNE

9

10

11

12

13

JUNE

14

15

16

17

18

JUNE

19

20

21

22

23

JUNE

24

25

26

27

28

29

30

1

2

3

JULY

4

5

6

7

8

JULY

9

10

11

12

13

JULY

14

15

16

17

18

JULY

19

20

21

22

23

JULY

24

25

26

27

28

JULY–AUGUST

29

30

31

1

2

AUGUST

3

4

5

6

7

AUGUST

8

9

10

11

12

AUGUST

13

14

15

16

17

AUGUST

18

19

20

21

22

AUGUST

23

24

25

26

27

AUGUST–SEPTEMBER

28

29

30

31

1

SEPTEMBER

2

3

4

5

6

SEPTEMBER

7

8

9

10

11

SEPTEMBER

12

13

14

15

16

SEPTEMBER

17

18

19

20

21

SEPTEMBER

22

23

24

25

26

27

28

29

30

1

OCTOBER

2

3

4

5

6

OCTOBER

7

8

9

10

11

OCTOBER

12

13

14

15

16

OCTOBER

17

18

19

20

21

OCTOBER

22

23

24

25

26

OCTOBER

27

28

29

30

31

NOVEMBER

1

2

3

4

5

NOVEMBER

6

7

8

9

10

NOVEMBER

11

12

13

14

15

NOVEMBER

16

17

18

19

20

NOVEMBER

21

22

23

24

25

NOVEMBER

26

27

28

29

30

DECEMBER

1

2

3

4

5

DECEMBER

6

7

8

9

10

DECEMBER

11

12

13

14

15

DECEMBER

16

17

18

19

20

DECEMBER

21

22

23

24

25

DECEMBER

26

27

28

29

30   31